'Twas the Night Before
Christmas
on Sesame
Street

123
SESAME STREET

sourcebooks
jabberwocky

By Lillian Jaine
Illustrated by Joe Mathieu

'Twas the night before Christmas, when all through the house not a creature was stirring, not even a Grouch.

The stockings were hung by the chimney with care,
in hopes that St. Nicholas soon would be there.

Cookie Monster was nestled all snug in his bed,
while visions of cookies danced in his head.

When out on the street there arose such a clatter,
he sprang from the bed to see what was the matter.

And what to his wondering eyes should appear,
but a miniature sleigh and eight tiny reindeer!

"Santa!" he cried. "Me think this is great!"
"But me wish me not eat what was on Santa's plate!"

"Oh no!" Cookie shouted. "What should me do?"
He must make more cookies for Santa, he knew.
So he flew to the kitchen, this time not to eat,
but to make sure he left his friend Santa a treat!

FLOUR

Sugar

BAKING POWDER

VANILLA

MERRY CHRISTMAS COOKIE!

Merry Christmas uncle Cookie!

There was so much to do and no time to waste,
and Cookie was worried by all that he faced.

If only he had an elf helper or two,
then there would be nothing that he couldn't do.

Then the very next moment, Cookie heard a strange sound.
Santa? he thought, as he turned right around.

Not Santa, but better: 'twas all of his friends!
"We can help," Elmo said, "from now till the end."

Elmo started to mix, then measure and splatter.
(And though Bert was the baker, Ernie tasted some batter.)

The clock ticked away, and when the bell sounded,
they opened the oven, pleased and astounded!

The Count frosted cookies, then counted each one,
and Abby got all of the sprinkling done.

"Hooray!" Cookie cried, his plate filled to the brim.
Now Santa had treats that were ready for him!

And then, in a twinkling,
they heard on the roof
the prancing and pawing
of each reindeer hoof.

They set out the cookies, and as they turned 'round,
down the chimney St. Nicholas came with a bound!

His eyes, how they twinkled! His dimples, how merry!
His cheeks were like roses, his nose like a cherry!

He had a broad face and a little round belly
that shook when he laughed, like a bowlful of jelly!

He spoke not a word,
but went straight to his work,
and filled all the stockings,
then turned with a jerk.

The cookies—he saw them! Right next to the tree!
"Oh boy!" Cookie whispered. "Me sure hope he's hungry!"

Santa took a big bite,
and then smiled so wide
that our dear Cookie Monster
was beaming with pride.

"We did it!" he whispered, and hugged all his friends.
"Me thank you, again and again and again!"

And now all the friends were as pleased as could be.
Santa ate not just one cookie, but three!

Then laying his finger aside of his nose,
and giving a nod, up the chimney he rose!

He sprang to his sleigh, to his team gave a whistle,
and away they all flew like the down of a thistle.

But they heard him exclaim,
as he drove out of sight,
"Merry Christmas, Sesame Street,
and to all a good night!"

Cookie Monster's Christmas Sugar Cookie Recipe

Have an adult preheat the oven to 350 degrees.

INGREDIENTS FOR COOKIES

- 1 **cup butter or margarine**
- 2 **cups granulated sugar**
- 1 **tsp. vanilla**
- 2 **eggs (or egg substitute)**
- 4 **cups flour**
- 2 **tsp. baking powder**
- ½ **tsp. salt**

INGREDIENTS FOR FROSTING

- 8 **oz. cream cheese, room temperature**
- 4 **tbsp. unsalted butter (½ stick), at room temperature**
- 1 **lb. powdered sugar**
- 1 **tbsp. vanilla extract**
   Decorations of your choice

DIRECTIONS

1. Combine ingredients in a large mixing bowl. Beat on medium speed until smooth.
2. Chill dough in fridge for 30 minutes, then roll out and cut using a cookie cutter (try a Christmas tree cookie cutter!).
3. Bake at 350 degrees for 8–10 minutes or till desired color. Have an adult take the cookies out of the oven.
4. While cookies cool, create frosting by beating cream cheese and butter until smooth and combined. Slowly add powdered sugar, a cup at a time, beating after each addition until combined. Add vanilla extract.
5. Frost and top with decorations (try green or red sugar sprinkles!).
6. Enjoy!

"Sesame Workshop,"® "Sesame Street,"® and associated characters, trademarks, and design elements are owned and licensed by Sesame Workshop. Copyright © 2014 Sesame Workshop. All rights reserved.

Cover and internal design © 2014 by Sourcebooks, Inc.

Cover illustrations © Sesame Workshop
Cover design by Jason Lavicky
Text by Lillian Jaine
Illustrations by Joe Mathieu

Sourcebooks and the colophon are registered trademarks of Sourcebooks, Inc.

Published by Sourcebooks Jabberwocky, an imprint of Sourcebooks, Inc.
P.O. Box 4410, Naperville, Illinois 60567-4410
(630) 961-3900
Fax: (630) 961-2168
www.jabberwockykids.com

Library of Congress Cataloging-in-Publication data is on file with the publisher

Source of Production: Worzalla, Stevens Point WI, USA
Date of Production: August 2014
Run Number: 5002111

Printed and bound in the United States of America.
WOZ 10 9 8 7 6 5 4 3 2 1